PATCHWORK TALES

Susan L. Roth and Ruth Phang

ATHENEUM   1984   NEW YORK

ACKNOWLEDGEMENTS

Our thanks to Charlotte Berman, Ruth Cahrmann, the Cheshire Cat Bookstore, Mrs. Covington and Mrs. Nelson at Noyes Library, Karen Day, Deborah Fleming, Gloria Kamen, Jean Karl, Marie Evelyne Lamour, Thomas and Eva Laufer, Jan Stiny, and Sue Valle for all their help to us on this project.

Library of Congress Cataloging in Publication Data

Phang, Ruth.   Patchwork tales.

SUMMARY: Grandmother tells her granddaughter the family stories behind the various blocks in a patchwork quilt. Illustrated with wood block prints of the quilt patches and including instructions for making a small patchwork quilt.
[1. Quilts—Fiction. 2. Patchwork—Fiction. 3. Family life—Fiction] I. Roth, Susan. II. Title.
PZ7.P44877Pat 1984   [E]   84-2987
ISBN 0-689-31053-6

Text and pictures copyright © 1984 by Ruth Phang and Susan Roth
Published simultaneously in Canada by
McClelland & Stewart, Ltd.
Composition by Dix Typesetters, Inc. Syracuse, New York
Printed and bound by
the Worzalla Publishing Company, Stevens Point, Wisconsin
Typography by Mary Ahern
First Edition

With love to
M & D, JR, & AAA
Mom & Dad, J, S, L, & E

This grandma's quilt is a typical sampler. Each of the patterns is a traditional design. Sometimes quilt block titles were obvious descriptions of the designs; other times the titles seemed more fanciful. Historically, some quilters did incorporate meaningful bits of old clothing into their quilts to tell their patchwork stories.

"Grandma, tell me
the patchwork quilt stories
before I go to sleep."

GRANNY'S STAR

"I made the middle square when I was a little girl like you. My grandma helped me."

"*Your* grandma!"

"Yes, she would have been your great-great grandma."

"What would *her* grandma have been to me?"

"Your great-great-great-great grandma, I suppose."

BRIDAL WREATH

"This one came from my wedding dress—the dress I wore when Grandpa and I got married."

"Did you have a fancy wedding with lots of flowers and a big cake with a bride and groom standing on the top?"

"Sure we did."

"Were you holding hands with Grandpa? Were you in love?"

"We're *still* in love!"

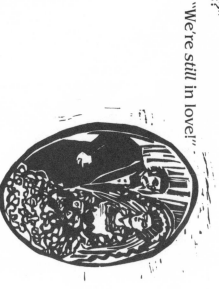

PINE TREE

"You know the big pine tree right in our front yard. I have a picture of your mommy planting it in her farmer's overalls. My patchwork tree is made out of those overalls.

"You can see your mommy grew a lot since that day."

"But not as much as the pine tree!"

FISH BLOCK

"Tell me the one when Mommy fell into the lake in her red velvet dress."

"She was showing her visitors the minnows in the lake. She was sure that she could catch one for her friends. The rocks were so slippery that she fell right in with the minnows."

"Was it deep?"

"No, just wet. And so was the red velvet dress. The fish in this block are made out of the very same red velvet."

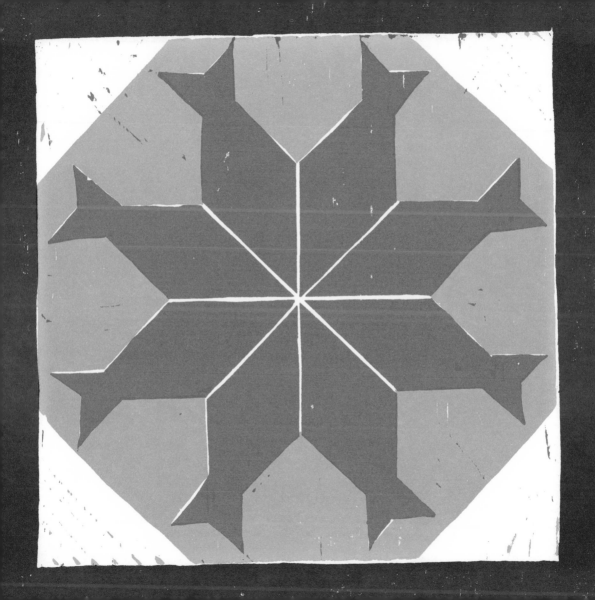

CORN AND BEANS

"Your mommy always loved to cook. She graduated from mudpies and concocted this recipe. We bravely tasted the biscuits she made, but we had great difficulty swallowing them. Your mommy was so insulted, she tore off her apron. (There it is, in this patchwork square.) She threw it on the floor, and she ran out of the room screaming, 'You don't like my cooking!' "

"I like the biscuits she makes for me!"

SUNBONNET GIRL

"What about the sunbonnet girl?"

"That dress was part of your mommy's dress, and that's what your mommy looked like to me when I made the quilt."

"Oh, Grandma. This sunbonnet girl even has golden hair."

"So did your mommy when she was very young."

"Mommy's hair is darker than mine now!"

"Golden hair almost always gets darker as the person gets older—unless it gets whiter."

"Yours looks like silver."

"Thank you. But it's just hair."

LEAP FROG

"You know how all children put on plays for grown-ups. Can you imagine that your mommy insisted on being the frog instead of the princess? She just loved the green frog suit. Everyone agreed she was the best frog they had ever seen.

"Do you see how one strip in the pattern goes over then under another? Just like when you play leap frog."

SCHOOLHOUSE

"This is from the dress your mommy wore on her first day of school. She didn't want to go into her classroom. When she got there, she held onto me and cried. There was another little girl who was crying even harder than your mommy. All of a sudden the girls noticed each other. They started laughing instead of crying, and they became fast friends."

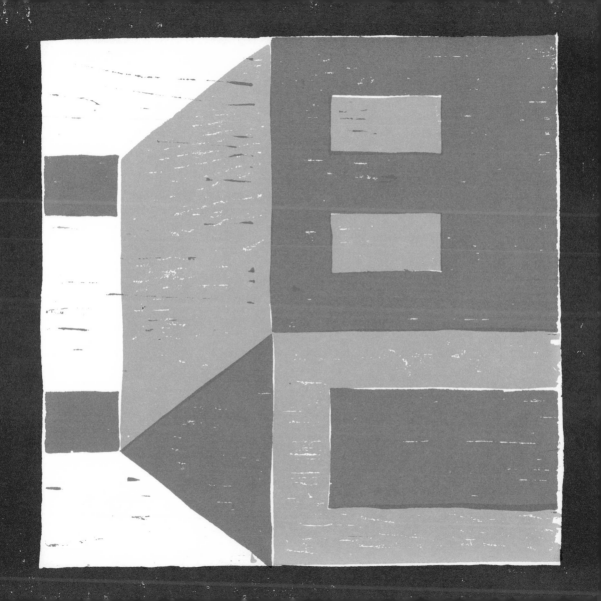

BEAR'S PAW

"One time when we were on a camping trip, I discovered that someone had been in our picnic basket. Grandpa was sure that a bear had visited us. I was ready to go home until we found that our bear was really your mommy. She had chocolate cake crumbs all over her sleeping bag and chocolate icing all over her sleepy smile.

"'She must have been hungry as a bear,' Grandpa said. "'I cut the bear's paws in this square from that little sleeping bag.'"

"The back of the quilt is a big mess."

"That's not a mess; it's called crazy quilt. I used up all my scraps for the crazy quilt back. They used to do that in the olden days all the time."

"When you made this quilt, it *was* the olden days."

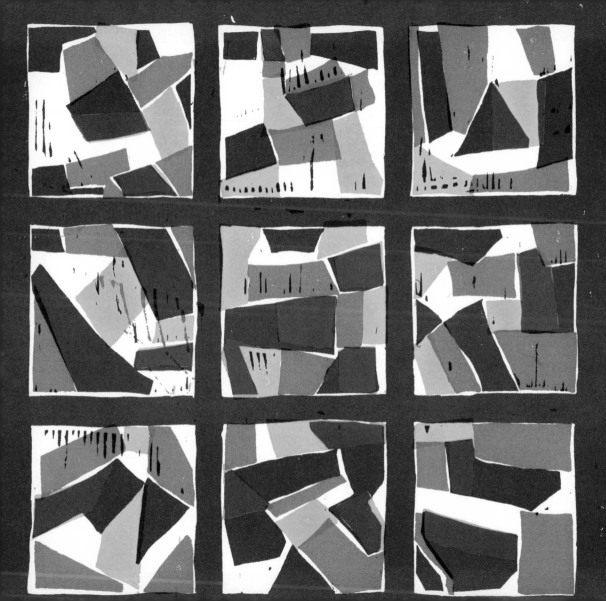

"Grandma, would you make a quilt just for me? Full of *my* stories?"

"Let's make one together."

"I'll tell you the stories I want in my quilt."

"But you're supposed to be sleeping now. Snuggle under your mommy's quilt, all cozy and warm, and tomorrow we'll get started.

Good night."

1

To make your first quilt, make a simple one of plain squares. For a doll's size quilt you will need:

3

needles
pins
thread
matching double-fold
   quilt binding, one
     package
scissors
cotton or wool yarn
an adult to help you

2

nine squares of material, each the size of this page plus ½ inch seam allowance
batting, 21 inches
   square
one piece of material 21 inches square for the backing

4

Arrange your squares into three rows of three across.

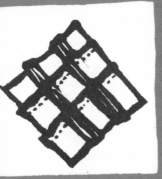

5

Sew the pieces within each row together, right sides together, ½-inch seam. Press seams to one side, preferably toward the darker color. Do all three rows this way.

6
Then sew the rows together, again with ½-inch seams. Press seams to one side.

9
Pin quilt binding all around the edges and sew on, catching all the layers within.

7
Sandwich your quilt together, with the batting (or filling) between the patched top and the backing. Baste.

8
Trim to fit.

10
Use yarn to tie the quilt, in the middle of each square, through all three layers. Use square knots, leaving one inch ends on top.

THE END